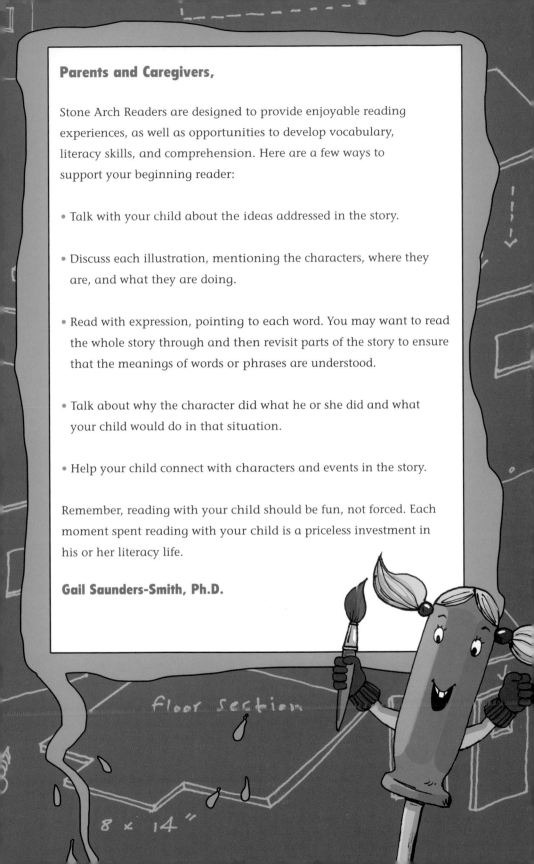

Parents and Caregivers,

Stone Arch Readers are designed to provide enjoyable reading experiences, as well as opportunities to develop vocabulary, literacy skills, and comprehension. Here are a few ways to support your beginning reader:

- Talk with your child about the ideas addressed in the story.

- Discuss each illustration, mentioning the characters, where they are, and what they are doing.

- Read with expression, pointing to each word. You may want to read the whole story through and then revisit parts of the story to ensure that the meanings of words or phrases are understood.

- Talk about why the character did what he or she did and what your child would do in that situation.

- Help your child connect with characters and events in the story.

Remember, reading with your child should be fun, not forced. Each moment spent reading with your child is a priceless investment in his or her literacy life.

Gail Saunders-Smith, Ph.D.

Stone Arch Readers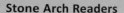

are published by Stone Arch Books
a Capstone Imprint
151 Good Counsel Drive, P.O. Box 669
Mankato, Minnesota 56002
www.capstonepub.com

Library of Congress Cataloging-in-Publication Data
Klein, Adria F. (Adria Fay), 1947-
  Sophie Screwdriver / by Adria Klein ; illustrated by Andrew Rowland.
      p. cm. — (Stone Arch readers. Tool school)
  Summary: The new school playground has arrived, and Sophie Screwdriver
is ready to make sure everything is safe.
ISBN 978-1-4342-3044-7 (library binding)
ISBN 978-1-4342-3386-8 (pbk.)
  [1. Tools—Fiction. 2. Playgrounds—Fiction. 3. Repairing—Fiction. 4. Helpfulness—
Fiction.] I. Rowland, Andrew, 1962- ill. II. Title.
  PZ7.K678324So 2011
  [E]—dc22
                            2010050217

Reading Consultants:
Gail Saunders-Smith, Ph.D.
Melinda Melton Crow, M.Ed.
Laurie K. Holland, Media Specialist

Cover Concept: Russel Griesmer
Art Director/Designer: Kay Fraser
Production Specialist: Michelle Biedscheid

Printed in the United States of America in Melrose Park, Illinois.
032011
006112LKF11

Sophie Screwdriver

by Adria Klein

illustrated by Andy Rowland

MEET THE
TOOL
TEAM

Tia Tape Measure

Hank Hammer

floor section

8 x 14"

Sammy Saw   **Sophie Screwdriver**

Sophie jumps and twirls. She twirls and jumps.

"Hurry! Hurry! Hurry!" she says,
"There is so much to do!"

All the tools come running.

"What's going on?" asks Sammy.

"The new playground is here!"
says Sophie.

"Hooray!" says Hank.

"We need to make sure
everything is safe," says Sophie.

"That's a big job," says Tia.

"It sure is!" says Sophie.

"We are going to be busy,"
says Sammy.

"Let's get started," says Hank.

"I can't wait!" says Sophie.

Sophie runs to the swings.

"This seat is loose. I can fix it," says Sophie.

"Turn, turn, turn. Now it is safe," she says.

Sophie runs to the slide.

"This slide step is loose. I can fix it," says Sophie.

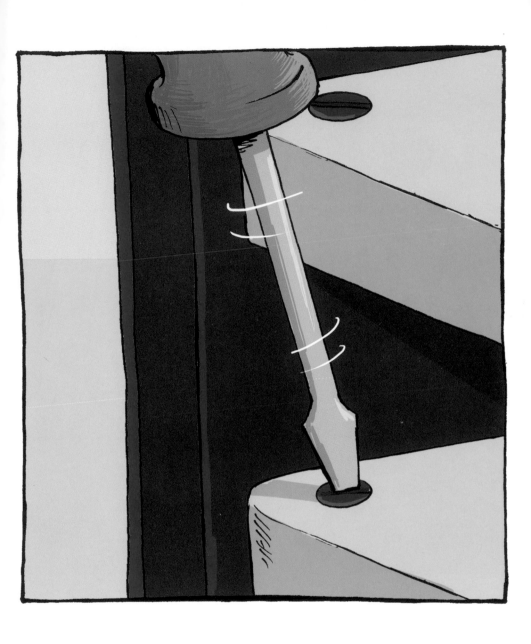

"Turn, turn, turn. Now it is safe," she says.

"Slow down, Sophie," says Tia.

"How can we help?" asks Sammy.

"I'm not sure," says Sophie.

"What's left to fix?" asks Hank.

"I bet we can fix the climbing
wall together," says Sammy.

"Good idea!" says Sophie.

"Tia, you can measure the
distance between the handles,"
says Sophie.

"No problem," says Tia.

"Hank, you can hammer the
handles on tight," says Sophie.

"No problem," says Hank.

"What can I do?" asks Sammy.

"I have the perfect job for you,"
says Sophie.

"What is it?" asks Sammy.

"You can test the new climbing wall!" says Sophie.

"Hooray!" says Sammy. "Fixing things is fun!"

"And we're done just in time," says Sophie.

STORY WORDS

twirls

measure

playground

distance

safe

handles

Total Word Count: 237

STONE ARCH READERS · LEVEL 2 · TOOL SCHOOL

Tia Tape Measure

STONE ARCH READERS · LEVEL 2 · TOOL SCHOOL

Sammy Saw

STONE ARCH READERS · LEVEL 2 · TOOL SCHOOL

Hank Hammer

TOOL SCHOOL